Karen's Sleepover

**Here are some other books
about Karen
that you might enjoy:**

Little Sister

Karen's Sleepover
Ann M. Martin

Illustrations by Susan Tang

A
LITTLE APPLE
PAPERBACK

SCHOLASTIC INC.
New York Toronto London Auckland Sydney

ISBN 0-590-43652-X

Copyright © 1990 by Ann M. Martin. All rights reserved. Published by Scholastic Inc. APPLE PAPERBACKS is a registered trademark of Scholastic Inc. BABY-SITTERS LITTLE SISTER is a trademark of Scholastic Inc.

12 11   5/9

Printed in the U.S.A.   40

First Scholastic printing, July 1990

This book
is in honor of the birth of
Emma Feiwel

Party Time

"Help! Help me! I'm lost! And a bear is after me!"

That was not true, of course. I was not lost, and no bear was after me. There are no bears in Stoneybrook, Connecticut. At least, I don't think there are any bears.

Hi. My name is Karen Brewer. I'm seven years old, which is a very good age. I have a little brother named Andrew, an adopted sister, a stepsister, and three stepbrothers. I wear glasses and I have some freckles. Once I got a horrible haircut, but now my

1

hair is grown out and back to normal. It is pretty long.

When I was shouting about the bear, I was in my father's backyard. I was playing with my two best friends, Hannie Papadakis and Nancy Dawes. We are all in Ms. Colman's second-grade class at Stoneybrook Academy. It was a Saturday afternoon and we were pretending we were camping. Nancy had said, "Let's play 'Going Camping.'" So we made a tent by draping a blanket over two chairs. Then Elizabeth, my stepmother, let us take some pots and pans out of the kitchen and put them in our tent. Now we were running around pretending we were in the woods.

"I'll save you!" Hannie yelled to me. "Hey, bear!" she cried. "Go away! Shoo!"

"You can't say 'shoo' to a bear!" exclaimed Nancy. "You say 'shoo' to a fly. Or maybe to a cat or even a small dog. But not to a bear."

"What do you say to a bear?" Hannie wondered.

2

Nancy did not know.

"Well, I'm tired," I said. "I think it is bedtime."

My friends and I made beds out of piles of leaves. Then we lay down in the leaves. They got stuck in our hair and on our sweaters.

"I wish we had real sleeping bags out here," said Hannie.

"That would be so, so cool," I agreed.

"I have a real sleeping bag, but it's at my house," said Nancy. (Nancy does not live nearby. She lives next door to Mommy's house.)

"We have real sleeping bags, too," I said, "but they're in our attic. The last time we used them was when Kristy had a sleep-over." (Kristy is my big stepsister.)

"Sleepovers sound like fun," said Hannie. "I have never, ever been to one."

"Me, neither," said Nancy and I at the same time.

"I bet you get to do all sorts of great things at a sleepover," said Hannie.

"The sleeping-bag part would be really fun," I added.

"Yeah," said Nancy.

"Do you think we're too young to go to a sleepover?" asked Hannie.

"Of course not!" I said. "Seven is old enough to do anything!"

"You can't drive when you're seven," said Nancy.

"Noooo. But you could have a sleepover. . . . And I'm going to have one!" I said suddenly.

"You *are?*" cried Hannie and Nancy.

"Yes. Yes, I am. I will have one right here at Daddy's house — if Daddy and Elizabeth say I can."

"Wow!" said Hannie.

Later that day, Hannie walked home, and Mrs. Dawes picked Nancy up. When my friends were gone, I found Daddy and Elizabeth. They were in the kitchen.

"Um, I have something to ask you," I said to them.

"What is it?" asked Daddy.

"Can I have a sleepover party for my friends? And can I have it here?"

Daddy and Elizabeth looked at each other. They were talking with their eyes. At last Daddy said, "I don't see why not."

"All *right!*" I shouted.

The Two-Twos

Late Sunday afternoon, Mommy came to pick up Andrew and me, and take us to her house.

Toot, toot! went her car horn in the driveway.

"Mommy's here," I said.

" 'Bye! Good-bye!" called Andrew and I. There was a lot of hugging and kissing when we left Daddy's house. "See you in two weeks!" I called.

The reason Mommy and Daddy live in different houses is because they're divorced.

7

First they were married, then they had
Andrew and me, then they decided to get
divorced. They wanted to live in separate
houses.

Guess what. After awhile, they each got
married again. Daddy married Elizabeth.
She already had four kids of her own. They
are Sam and Charlie, who go to high school;
David Michael, who is seven like me; and
Kristy, who is thirteen. Kristy is one of my
most favorite people. She likes to baby-sit,

and she is even the president of a business called The Baby-sitters Club. I like it best when Kristy baby-sits for *me!* Sam, Charlie, David Michael, and Kristy are my stepbrothers and stepsister.

Andrew and I also have an adopted sister. Her name is Emily Michelle and she's two years old. She came all the way from a country called Vietnam. Daddy and Elizabeth wanted Emily very much. I am still deciding if I like her. She is my little sister and Kristy is my big sister. I'm the middle sister.

It is a good thing Daddy has lots and lots of money, because his family sure is big. There is Nannie, too. She's Elizabeth's mother and she helps take care of us. Plus, there is Boo-Boo, Daddy's fat old mean cat, and Shannon, David Michael's puppy.

At Mommy's house there are just Mommy and Seth (he's our stepfather), Rocky and Midgie, Seth's cat and dog, and Emily Junior, my rat, who is named after Emily Michelle. Oh, and there are Andrew and me, of course. We live with Mommy and Seth most of the time. We only live at Daddy's every other weekend and for two weeks during the summer.

Daddy's house is big. Mommy's is little.

Since Andrew and I live at two houses, I call us the two-twos. I got the name from a book Ms. Colman read to our class once. It was called *Jacob Two-Two Meets the Hooded Fang.* I thought "two-two" was the perfect name for Andrew and me. We are Andrew Two-Two and Karen Two-Two because we have two of almost everything. We have two houses. We have two families. We have two dogs, one at the little house and one at the big house. We have two cats, one at each house. I have a best friend at each house. We have clothes and toys and books and bicycles at each house. This makes going back and forth much easier. We hardly ever have to pack anything. I even have two stuffed cats, Moosie and Goosie. Moosie stays in my room at the big house. Goosie stays in my room at the little house.

10

Being a two-two is not always easy, though. For instance, I only had one special blanket — Tickly. I kept leaving Tickly at one house or the other. Finally I had to rip Tickly in half so I'd be sure to have a piece at each house. And there is only one Emily Junior. I miss her a lot when I'm at the big house, even though I know Mommy and Seth take good care of her.

Here's one nice thing about being a two-two. I like the little house for peace and quiet, and I *love* the big house for excitement. I am lucky to have both. I wish Mommy and Daddy were still married, but being a two-two isn't all bad.

A Real Sleepover

"Guess what! Guess what!" I cried as soon as I ran into Ms. Colman's class on Monday morning.

"Indoor voice. Use your indoor voice, Karen," Ms. Colman reminded me. She was sitting at her desk. A lot of kids were in our room, but school had not started yet.

"Okay," I said to Ms. Colman. "Sorry."

I like Ms. Colman a lot. She is nice to me. I am the youngest kid in my class (I skipped most of first grade), and I have to wear *two* pairs of glasses — one for reading and one for the rest of the time. Ms. Colman helps me to remember things, like which pair of glasses to wear and when to use my indoor voice.

She never yells.

"Hannie! Nancy!" I said in a loud whisper.

"What?" they answered.

"Daddy told me I could have a sleepover party!"

I had known that since Saturday, but I had kept it a secret. I thought it might be a nice surprise for Monday morning. And it was.

"You're kidding!" exclaimed Nancy.

"Really?" cried Hannie.

We were all whispering excitedly.

"What's the secret?" asked Natalie Springer. She walked over to us.

I looked at Hannie and Nancy. Should I tell Natalie? After all, I hadn't decided who to invite to my sleepover yet — except for my two best friends.

Hannie and Nancy shrugged. So I said

grandly, "I'm having a sleepover party . . . and *you're* invited!" Daddy and Elizabeth had said I could invite ten people to my sleepover.

"Thanks!" said Natalie.

Then I heard a voice behind me. It was a high-pitched boy's voice. "I'm having a sleepover party . . . and *you're* invited!" I knew it was Ricky Torres and he was imitating me.

I also know he was just teasing.

"Puh-*lease* can I come to your sleepover?" kidded Ricky. "I'll bring my best nightgown and — "

"Sleepovers are for girls," I informed him. "At least, mine is."

"For all girls?" asked Ricky.

"For all the girls in our class," I told him. I hadn't thought about it, but that seemed like a nice thing to do. I would invite all the girls in my class. There were nine of us. I liked the girls. And if I invited every one of them, then nobody would feel left out.

"I'm coming, too," said Ricky. "I am going to crash your party."

"No, you're not," I told him, even though I would not have minded if he had. Ricky and I like each other.

"Then I am going to come spy on your party. I am going to spy on you girls in your nightgowns."

"Eeee!" cried Nancy. "No!"

"What party?" asked Jannie Gilbert.

So I told her about the sleepover.

By the end of the day, every kid in Ms.

Colman's class knew about my party — and I hadn't even sent out invitations. Oh, well. Who cared? I would send invitations later anyway. For now, I was very happy. All the girls kept coming up to me and saying things like, "A *real* sleepover. Cool!" And, "Only my *big* sister ever goes to sleepovers. Now I can go, too!"

Nobody could wait for my sleepover party.

Party Plans

Eleven days later, Andrew and I were back at the big house for our weekend. On Friday night we played with David Michael and Emily. But on Saturday I had important things to do. I had to make plans for my sleepover party.

I decided to talk to Kristy. Kristy and her friends in the Baby-sitters Club have lots of sleepovers. Kristy would know what to do at a sleepover. She would also know what I would need to buy.

"Kristy?" I said.

Kristy was in her room. She was working at her desk. Kristy is in eighth grade and she gets lots of homework.

"Are you *very* busy?" I asked her.

Kristy put her pencil down. "Not too busy," she answered. "What's up? Do you need help with something?"

I nodded. "My sleepover party. What do I need to buy?"

"Mostly food," Kristy replied. She ripped a piece of paper out of her notebook. "Let's make a list." (We sat down together on her bed.)

"What kind of food?" I asked.

"Pizzas," Kristy said immediately. "They'll be for dinner. Then for snacks, you will need popcorn, potato chips, pretzels . . ." Kristy went on and on. We wrote everything down.

"Do we need any party decorations?" I asked.

Kristy shook her head. "Nope."

"We don't?" I must have looked awfully disappointed because Kristy let me add:

CREPE PAPER
and
BALLOONS

to the list. (The first time I spelled *crepe* like this: crape. Kristy helped me fix it.)

"Now," I said, "what do you *do* at a sleepover? I know you don't sleep."

"Well, you don't sleep much," Kristy replied, smiling. "You do lots of other things. You watch a spooky movie and scare yourselves. You make a batch of fudge."

"Can we make Slice 'n' Bake cookies instead?" I interrupted.

"Whatever. Then you gossip. You raid the refrigerator. And you stay up as late as you can. My friends and I always play Truth or Dare and try on makeup," added Kristy, "but I think you guys are too young for that."

"We are not!" I cried, but I didn't really care. "Boy," I said. "We'll have an awful lot to do at the party. Thank you, Kristy."

19

I gave Daddy the list that Kristy and I had made. Then I went to my room and finished making the invitations for the party. They said:

Come to a sleepover! Bring your sleeping bag! (Let me know if you don't have one.) We will watch a movie. We will eat pizza. We will make cookies. Maybe we will try on make up.

Then I wrote down the place and time of the party so my friends would know where and when the sleepover would be held. When the invitations were finished, I slipped them in the mailbox on our street. Then I came home.

"David Michael, Andrew," I said, when I found them playing in the family room. "You have to stay away from my party. No boys allowed."

Then I found Sam and told him the same thing. Sam told me I was a weirdo. I ignored him.

Then I found Charlie and told *him* the same thing, but I asked if he would tell us a ghost story and then leave the party as soon as he was done.

"Sure," said Charlie.

Oh, boy! I thought. This is going to be the best sleepover ever!

Nancy's Invitation

I had mailed my invitations on Saturday. By Wednesday, every girl in Ms. Colman's class had received one — except Nancy.

Nancy looked insulted. She looked hurt. "Didn't you send me an invitation?" she asked.

"Of course I did," I told her. "I mailed it with the other invitations. I mailed them all at the same time. I bet yours got lost in the mail. Wait a couple more days. Anyway, you know you're invited to the party whether you get your invitation or not."

"But I *want* an invitation!" Nancy demanded.

"I'm sure it will be waiting for you when you get home from school today," I told her.

It wasn't.

It wasn't there on Thursday afternoon, either.

When Nancy's mother drove Nancy and me to school on Friday morning, Nancy scowled the whole way. Then she waited until we were in our classroom. She waited until Hannie and some other girls were around us and she said, "I guess Karen did not invite me after all. I guess she never mailed me an invitation. She doesn't want me at her sleepover. And I even have my own sleeping bag. I would not need to borrow one."

"I do too want you at my party!"

I almost yelled that, but I remembered about indoor and outdoor voices. So I didn't say it too loudly.

"You don't mean that," said Nancy. She

23

looked embarrassed. Then she looked sad. "I am the only girl in the class that you didn't invite. And I thought I was one of your best friends."

"You *are*," I told her, just as Ms. Colman said, "Time to take your seats, class."

I couldn't talk to Nancy anymore. She and Hannie sit in the back row. I sit in the front row with Ricky Torres and Natalie Springer. This is because we wear glasses. No one else in our class does.

And now I know why Nancy doesn't need them. She must have eyes like an eagle. Otherwise, from way in the back of the room, how could she have seen me doodling in my math book later on? But she did.

She raised her hand.

"Yes, Nancy?" said Ms. Colman.

"Karen's drawing in her book," Nancy announced.

Ms. Colman looked down at my book where I had drawn:

"Have you finished your work, Karen?" Ms. Colman asked me.

I shook my head. "No," I said in a tiny voice. I wanted to turn around and give Nancy a mean look, but I couldn't. Ms. Colman was standing right next to me.

"Are you having trouble with the work?" asked Ms. Colman.

"No."

"You know you are not supposed to draw in books, don't you?"

"Yes," I replied. My voice was getting smaller and smaller.

"Then you will have to stay inside during recess today," said Ms. Colman. Stay inside! Ms. Colman had never punished me before. "You will have to erase your drawings and

then think about what you did," she told me.

"Okay," I said.

"And Nancy," Ms. Colman went on. "No more tattling, please."

"Okay," said Nancy. "I'm sorry." But she did not look sorry. Especially when she got to go to recess after lunch and I had to go back to our classroom. She looked sort of happy about that.

Nancy was *really* mad at me.

"You're Un-invited!"

Nancy and I did not speak to each other during the rest of school that day. When she looked at me, I would turn my head away. When I looked at her, she would do the same thing.

I was very upset. Hardly anyone ever had to miss recess. And I was sure Ms. Colman was angry with me, even though she didn't act angry.

The thing was, I knew I should not have been drawing in my book. You are not supposed to do that. Unless it is a coloring book, or maybe a workbook. But not a real book. So I *had* done something wrong.

But Nancy had tattled on me. If I had seen *her* drawing in *her* book, I would not have tattled. I might have whispered, "Stop that, Nancy," (if I were sitting near her). I might have said, "It isn't nice to draw in books." But I would not have tattled.

Nancy and I did not have to ride home from school together that day. It was a good thing. I was mad at Nancy — and she was *still* mad at me because she hadn't gotten her invitation.

After school that day, I felt terrible. I couldn't even look forward to going to Daddy's. Andrew and I were not going there until next weekend. But guess what would happen then. The sleepover! Next Saturday night would be my sleepover. But thinking about the sleepover did not make me feel much better.

When our phone rang, I said, "I'll get it!" Maybe it would be Kristy. Talking to Kristy might make me feel better.

I picked up the phone. "Hello?" I said.

"Hi!" cried a voice.

The voice sounded like Nancy's, but it couldn't be.

"Who is this, please?" I asked politely.

"It's *me*, dumbbell. It's Nancy."

Why was Nancy calling?

"Yeah?" I said.

"Guess what?!" Nancy sounded gigundo excited.

"What?"

"It came! It came! The invitation to your sleepover came this afternoon!"

"Good."

"Karen, I — I'm sorry I got you in trouble today. Honest. I was just mad about the invitation. I promise I'll never tell on you again."

I didn't say anything.

"Okay?" Nancy went on. "I'm *really sorry*. But thank you, thank you, thank you for

inviting me. So — what can I bring to the party?"

"Nothing," I replied. "You're not invited after all. I un-invite you. People who get me in trouble with Ms. Colman do *not* come to my sleepovers." I hung up the phone.

Then I ran to my room. Part of me felt pleased. Now I had made Nancy feel as bad as she had made me feel. The other part of me felt awful. I did not like feeling bad, so

Nancy must not like feeling bad, either. And I had made her feel bad.

I did not know what to think. My thoughts were spinning around and around. Nancy was my best friend. How mad could best friends get? What if we never, ever spoke to each other again?

I almost called Nancy back. I almost said, "I'm sorry I un-invited you. Now you are re-invited. You can come after all."

But I just could not do that. Nancy had gotten me in trouble at school. And a best friend is not supposed to do that.

Best Enemies

All that weekend, Nancy and I stayed mad at each other. On Saturday, I invited Hannie over to play. On Sunday, Nancy invited Hannie over to play. But the three of us did not play together.

On Monday, school started again. Nancy was supposed to ride to Stoneybrook Academy with me, but I did not want her to. Anyway, she told her mother she would never ride in the same car with me again. Not in her whole life.

On Tuesday the same thing happened.

We did not say one word to each other. Mommy talked to me about it.

"Karen," she said, "sometimes best friends fight, but that does not mean they will never be best friends again."

"I guess," I said.

"And sometimes," Mommy went on, "when best friends fight, they hurt each other's feelings. You and Nancy don't want to do that, do you?"

"We already have," I told her. "Anyway, Nancy and I are not best friends. We are best enemies."

Mommy did not look happy to hear that.

In school, my sleepover was practically the only thing the girls talked about. Except for Nancy, because she was un-invited.

"I can't wait until Saturday!" exclaimed Jannie Gilbert at recess.

"Me, neither," said Natalie. "I am going to borrow my sister's sleeping bag. I don't have one of my own."

"I have one," said Leslie Morris.

"Me, too," said Hannie and Natalie and several other girls.

"I don't have one," said Jannie. She looked upset.

"Don't worry," I told her. "We have extras."

"Karen, are your brothers going to be at the party?" asked Natalie.

"They might be at home, but they are *not* coming to the party," I replied.

"What if they play tricks on us?" asked Jannie. "What if they give us pepper chewing gum or leave a rubber snake in someone's sleeping bag?"

"Aughh!" shrieked Leslie. "A rubber snake!"

"They will not play tricks," I said. "I will not let them."

"*I* might play tricks," said Ricky. He had been tossing around a football with some other kids in our grade. Now he was standing with us girls. "You!" I cried. "You're not coming to my party. It's just for girls."

"Yes I am coming," teased Ricky. "And

35

I am going to throw stones at your window and scare you."

"No!" shrieked Hannie.

"And I'll bring a handful of rubber snakes."

"No!" shrieked Leslie.

"And then I will spy on you and see all you girls in . . . your underwear!"

I began to laugh. "You are not going to do those things, Ricky," I said. "And you know it."

Everyone else began to laugh, too.

Everyone except Nancy. She was just standing nearby. She was watching and listening. But she was not smiling or laughing. I knew she wanted to come to the party. I felt pretty sorry for her. It is not fun to be left out of anything. It makes you feel gigundo bad.

But how could I ask my best enemy to come to my sleepover?

The New Girl

You just never know about surprises. I guess that is why they are surprises.

We had a big surprise in Ms. Colman's class on Wednesday morning. The school bell had just rung. Hannie and I and everyone else ran for our seats. (Nancy and I were still not speaking.) I settled down. Next to me, Ricky settled down.

We smiled at each other.

That was a nice change. We used to throw spitballs instead. Then one of us would tell on the other. That was before we were friends.

Usually, Ms. Colman makes morning announcements or takes attendance first thing. That morning she said, "Class, I have a surprise. Today, a new student is going to join our class. I hope you will make her feel — "

And just then, the door to our room opened. In stepped a girl we had never seen before. She came in by herself. (If *I* were a new student somewhere, I would want Mommy or Daddy to come into the classroom with me. At least on the first day.)

Ms. Colman stood with the new girl in front of the room. She put her arm around her. "Boys and girls," she said, "this is Pamela Harding. She is going to be in our class. Karen, would you please show Pamela where the cubbies are? Mr. Fitzwater" (he's the janitor) "will be bringing in a desk and chair for Pamela in a few minutes. Until

then, Pamela, you may sit at my desk. Okay?"

Pamela nodded.

Lucky duck! I thought. No one else had ever sat at Ms. Colman's desk. I showed Pamela the cubbies. I waited while she took off her jacket and put her lunch box away.

Then Pamela sat at Ms. Colman's desk.

Ms. Colman said, "Pamela, maybe you could tell the class about yourself."

"My name is Pamela Harding," said Pamela right away. "My family just moved to Stoneybrook. My mother writes books and my father is a dentist. I have a sister. She is sixteen. She lets me wear her perfume."

I was awed. So were all the other girls. I sneaked a look back at Hannie. She raised her eyebrows at me.

A book writer and a dentist! And a sixteen-year-old sister who let Pamela borrow her perfume!

Besides all that, there was the way Pamela was dressed. I thought she looked cool. Kristy would say she looked trendy. She was wearing baggy pink overalls and a pink-and-white-striped shirt. On her feet were pink high-top sneakers *with the tongues rolled down.* But best of all, on her head was a pink hat. It was *not* a dumb knitted one like for snowy days. It was made of felt. Ms. Colman let her wear it indoors. It seemed to be part of the outfit.

No one knew what to make of Pamela. Us girls thought she was beautiful. We wanted her to be our friend. But Pamela didn't say much to us. At lunchtime, she sat by herself. So we moved over to her table.

Pamela still didn't say anything.

At last I said, "I am having a sleepover on Saturday, Pamela. All the girls in our class are coming. Can you come, too?"

Pamela shrugged. She was busy eating her sandwich. "Sure," she finally replied. "I guess so."

"Great!" I said. Then I narrowed my eyes at Nancy. If we had been speaking to each other, I would have said, "See? *She* did not need an invitation in the mail."

Party Day

Saturday! It had come at last! I was gigundo excited.

In the morning, I leaped out of bed. I did not even bother to kiss Moosie on the nose. I got dressed as fast as I could. Then I ran downstairs. I ran into the kitchen where Daddy and Elizabeth and Nannie and Emily were having breakfast.

"Okay!" I said. "Let's go shopping! We have to buy all the stuff on the lists. And we can*not* forget balloons. And we have to order the pizzas!"

"Whoa," said Daddy. "Calm down."

And Elizabeth added, "Sit down. And please eat your breakfast."

I tried, but I couldn't. "What if the stores run out of popcorn or balloons or something?" I asked.

Daddy said they wouldn't.

But as soon as the stores opened, Nannie took me shopping. She knew I could not wait one second longer. We rode downtown in her old car, which is named the Pink Clinker.

We bought everything we needed. The only thing I felt bad about was Nancy. Should I invite her? No. I just could not.

In the afternoon, Kristy helped me get ready for the party. We decided that my guests and I would sleep upstairs in the playroom. That would be fun. Kristy and I blew up balloons. We hung crepe paper and balloons all around the playroom. It looked so, so pretty.

When the room was ready, I decided that I should remind everyone how to behave. I did not want anyone in my family to do or say something awful in front of Pamela.

"David Michael," I said, "you better leave me and my friends alone."

"Don't worry," he replied. "I am not coming near a bunch of girls."

"Sam, Charlie," I said, "you leave us alone, too."

"Maybe I will and maybe I won't," teased Sam.

Charlie looked serious. "I will stay out of

your way except for the ghost story," he said.

"Thank you," I replied.

Then I turned to Andrew and Emily. "Andrew, please do not get shy or act like a baby. Emily, please do not dribble food out of your mouth."

Andrew gave me a Cross Look. Emily did not understand what I'd said.

I could tell that everyone in the big house was glad when the doorbell rang. That meant a guest had arrived. The party would start — and I would stop ordering people around.

Pamela

I flung open our front door. I was all set to say, "Hi, Hannie!" Since Hannie lives across the street, I was sure she would be my first guest.

But guess who was standing on our front porch?

Pamela Harding.

And she was dressed up in one of her cool outfits again. She was wearing black pants with pink pockets on the knees and pink cuffs at the ankles. And over her pants she was wearing a *dress* with a flared skirt.

In her hair was a headband with a fancy, frilly bow attached to it.

What was I wearing? I was wearing jeans, and a sweat shirt that said "Surrender Dorothy," just like in the movie *The Wizard of Oz*.

I thought I looked like a dork next to Pamela.

Sam must have thought so, too. He leaned over and whispered in my ear. He called me a dweeb.

I just hoped that the rest of my friends would be wearing jeans, too. Were you *supposed* to get dressed up for a sleepover? Kristy had not said so.

"Hi, Pamela," I said. "Come on in. You look really nice."

"Thank you," she replied.

She was carrying an overnight bag, but no sleeping bag.

"Oh," I said. "You didn't bring a sleeping bag. Well, that's all right. You can use one of ours."

"I won't need one," Pamela replied. "I

have *never* slept on the floor. I *have* to sleep in a bed."

I looked at Elizabeth, who had just come into the front hall. Elizabeth said, "I guess you can sleep in Karen's bed tonight."

Pamela looked relieved, but I felt worried. What if *all* my friends wanted to sleep in beds?

Luckily they didn't. Soon Hannie and Natalie and Jannie and Leslie and everyone had arrived. Most of them brought sleeping bags. The others wanted to borrow ours. And nobody else was dressed up. I felt better.

"Okay!" I said to my friends. "Let's go upstairs to the playroom. That's where we are going to sleep tonight. So bring all your stuff with you."

"To the *play*room?" repeated Pamela. "You have a playroom?"

I wished Nancy were with me then. She usually knows what to say. She would have said something funny to Pamela.

But *I* just said, "Yes, we have a playroom.

49

I have a little brother and sister."

My friends and I put our sleeping bags on the floor in the playroom. We arranged them in a circle, like the spokes of a wagon wheel.

Then we sat on our sleeping bags. (Pamela sat in a chair.) We opened our overnight bags.

"Look what I brought!" cried Leslie. She held up her nightgown. It had leopard spots and red fringe on it. "It's really for playing dress-up," she said.

We started to laugh.

"I brought — ta-dah! — my musical puppy," said Jannie. "Look. You push this button on his tummy and he moves his head. Plus, his eyes blink on and off, and a music box inside him plays 'How Much Is That Doggie in the Window?'"

Now we couldn't stop laughing. Except for Pamela, who had never started.

Suddenly — *squirt, squirt, squirt!*

Ew! We were getting sprayed. We were all wet!

50

David Michael was standing in the doorway to the playroom. He was aiming his
water pistol at us.

"Gotcha!" he shouted. Then he ran away.

"Aughh! Ew! Gross!" we shrieked.

My sleepover had started. But was it off
to a good start or a bad start? I was not
sure.

Spook Night

Elizabeth took David Michael's water pistol away from him. She told him not to bother us anymore. I thanked her. But I thought that some of my friends had liked his surprise attack.

Oh, well.

It was pizza time.

"Who's hungry?" I asked when everyone had finished drying off. (Pamela was making a big show of patting herself with a towel. I felt bad that David Michael had ruined her hair.)

"I am!" cried my friends.

Even Pamela said, "I am!" Then she asked, "What's for dinner?"

"Pizza!" I said excitedly.

"Yea!" yelled Hannie and Natalie and almost everyone.

But Pamela said, "Pizza gives me bad breath. I can't eat it."

"Oh. Maybe . . . maybe Elizabeth or Kristy can fix you something else," I replied.

So Hannie, Leslie, Natalie, and I went to the kitchen. We put paper plates and cups and napkins and two bottles of soda on a tray. Then we picked up the pizza boxes very, very carefully.

As we were leaving the kitchen, Leslie whispered to me, "Karen? Do you think Pamela is having fun?"

Before I could answer, Hannie said, "I think Pamela is . . . well, I don't think *she* is any fun. I feel kind of like a baby around her."

I did not know what to say. I felt the same way, but I didn't want to admit it.

54

Anyway, we had to stop talking about Pamela because we had almost reached the playroom again.

"Here we are!" I said.

Everyone was sitting on their sleeping bags again. (Well, except Pamela.) They made a mad grab for the pizzas and soda and began to eat in their laps.

"My big sister is making you a sandwich," I told Pamela. "Peanut butter and jelly. But only a little peanut butter, in case you're afraid it will stick to the roof of your mouth, or give you peanut-butter breath."

Hannie giggled. The other girls looked at Pamela warily. I think most of them still wanted her to like them. I bet Nancy wouldn't care, though, if she were here. And I wished she were. She would not stand for what Pamela was doing.

"Okay, time for a spooky movie," I said. (We have a VCR and a TV in our playroom.) "Guess what I chose to watch with our dinner."

"What?" asked Leslie.

"The Wizard of Oz!"

"Ooh, goody!" exclaimed Jannie. "The witch is so scary."

"So are the flying monkeys," said someone else.

From her chair, Pamela sighed. "That is a baby movie," she said.

"Is not!" said the rest of us.

I decided that Pamela did not count. We watched the movie and ate our pizza while Pamela combed her hair and ate the sandwich Kristy brought her.

My friends and I got scareder and

scareder. When Dorothy was trapped in the witch's castle and the face of the Wicked Witch of the West appeared in the crystal ball, Hannie even screamed.

And then . . . from outside . . . BLAM! A huge clap of thunder sounded.

All the rest of us began to scream, too. A storm was coming. A big one.

I could tell we were going to have a spook night.

The Ricky Torres
Dough Boy

During the rest of the movie, my friends just sat and stared. The pizza was eaten. The storm was coming. We were glued to the TV. We could not think of anything except the witch and her broomstick and her castle.

We were so, so scared.

Finally Dorothy woke up from her dream. She was saying, "There's no place like home. There's no place like home." That was when we all let out sighs of relief.

"Whew," said Leslie. "I didn't think she was going to make it."

"Haven't you ever seen the movie before?" asked Pamela.

"No," replied Leslie. "Have you?"

"Only about eighty-seven times. We own the movie."

"Well, so do we, but it still scares me," I said. I felt like sticking up for Leslie.

Boy, did I wish Nancy were at my party. If you think I have a big mouth, you should hear Nancy. She says whatever she wants. She told me once that this is because she plans to be an actress one day. She says it is good practice.

I turned off the VCR. "Who wants to make cookies?" I asked.

"What kind?" Hannie wanted to know.

"Slice 'n' Bake with chocolate chips."

"Oh, yum! That is the best kind!" cried Leslie. "You can slice them up — which is really easy. Or you can make them into shapes!"

We carried the empty pizza boxes and all our trash downstairs. We threw everything away. Then I called, "Kristy! Can you come help us bake cookies?"

"Sure!" she called back.

(I am not allowed to touch the stove or the oven. A grown-up has to do that for me.)

"How come your sister is baby-sitting you?" Pamela asked me.

"She is *not* baby-sitting. She's just helping," I told her.

Then I decided to ignore Pamela. I joined Hannie and Natalie, who were slicing cookies, but eating about every other slice.

There is just nothing like raw cookie dough.

Before we had even put a tray of slices in the oven, Leslie rolled some dough into a ball and threw it at Jannie. Jannie giggled and threw it back. Soon we were having a dough-ball fight. Even Kristy joined it. We were giggling and shrieking and running around. (Pamela sat at the kitchen table. Her chin rested in her hand. She looked bored out of her skull. She did not even move when a piece of dough hit her head.)

The next thing I knew, the fight was over. And Natalie was holding up something she had made. "Who does this look like?" she asked.

"Ricky Torres!" I said.

It *was* Ricky. We baked him with the other cookies. When the timer rang, we watched Kristy take the cookies out of the oven.

"Who wants to eat Ricky?" she asked.

At first, no one could bear to eat the Ricky Torres Dough Boy. Finally Hannie said, "I'll eat him." She bit his head off.

"Aughh!" cried Kristy from behind her. "That hurt!"

Everyone laughed. Pamela looked bored. So I began to feel bad.

Kristy pulled me aside. "Are you having fun?" she asked me.

I shook my head. "No. Pamela Harding is ruining everything. . . . I wish Nancy were here."

"Please Come to My Sleepover!"

"**K**aren?" said Kristy. She had taken me into the den. My party guests were in the kitchen. They were eating the Slice 'n' Bake cookies and drinking milk.

"Yes?" I answered.

"Where *is* Nancy? Did she get sick or something?"

I sighed. "No. We had a fight."

"About what?"

"Nancy didn't get her invitation in the mail when everyone else did. She thought

I had not invited her to my party. So she was mad and she tattled on me and got me in trouble with Ms. Colman. *Then* Nancy got her invitation. She called and said she wasn't mad anymore. But *I* was. So I uninvited her. We have not spoken to each other for a whole week."

"Wow," said Kristy. "That was a big fight. I bet you wish it were over now, don't you?"

"Do I ever! I really need Nancy here. She would know what to do about Pamela. But what I really want is to make up with Nancy. I don't know how to do that, though. And I feel funny inviting her to my party *now*."

"I think you should call her," said Kristy. "Apologize to her. She already apologized to you. And say you forgive her for getting you in trouble. She was just angry then, Karen. People do all sorts of things when they are angry. And I bet Nancy would rather come to your party late than not at all."

I thought about that. "I don't know. Maybe. . . ."

"*Call* her," said Kristy. "It is the mature thing to do."

Well. I am a very mature person for a seven-year-old. So I said, "Okay. I will call her."

Kristy left the den so I could have some privacy. She said she would help my friends make more cookies.

My heart pounded as I dialed the phone. Mrs. Dawes answered.

"Hi," I said in a small voice. "This is Karen. Is Nancy there?"

"Sure. Hold on a sec."

As soon as Nancy got on the phone I started talking. I wanted to get things over with quickly. Like ripping a Band-Aid off fast instead of peeling it back slowly.

"Nancy, I'm really sorry I un-invited you to my party," I said. "But you made me feel bad when you got me in trouble. I know you feel bad now, though. So I think our fight should be over. And I want you to come to my party right away."

"You do? Thanks! And Karen, I *am* sorry I got you in trouble. That was a mean thing to do. Do you forgive me?"

"Oh, yes!" I said, remembering what Kristy had told me. "I forgive you. Do *you* forgive *me?*"

"Yes, I do."

"Good. Then come over right away. You

won't believe Pamela. She is making us all feel like babies."

"She is? How?"

"She thought *The Wizard of Oz* was not a scary movie, when everyone knows it is. I mean, duh. And she will not sleep in a sleeping bag. And she would not eat pizza with us. She said it gives her bad breath. Now she is just sitting while everyone else makes cookies. She looks like she thinks we are jerks. Maybe even dweebs. She is ruining everything. Please come to my sleepover. I really need you!"

So of course Nancy got permission from her parents. Her father said he would drive her right over.

Blackout

Flash! Flash! BLAM! BLAM!

Lightning lit up our yard. Thunder thundered. The storm was on its way — but there was no rain yet.

The rain did not start until Nancy arrived. She ran to our door and rang the bell three times fast. Just as she had climbed out of her daddy's car, the rain had begun to fall in huge, gusty sheets.

When I opened the door, though, Nancy was only a little wet. But she wanted to get inside fast.

" 'Bye!" she called to her father.

Mr. Dawes waved. Then he drove away.

I closed the door behind Nancy. We hugged tightly. Hannie smiled at us. She was glad our fight was over.

"Here," I said to Nancy. "Let me take your stuff. Hey, how come you brought two sleeping bags?" Nancy was wearing a knapsack and had been carrying a sleeping bag in each hand.

(Flash! BLAM!)

"Yeah," said Jannie. "How come?" Everybody had rushed into the front hall to greet Nancy.

"I heard that Pamela doesn't have a sleeping bag, so I brought one for her."

I tried not to giggle. So did Hannie and Natalie.

"I *sleep* in *beds*," was all Pamela would say.

"How boring," replied Nancy. Without waiting for Pamela to reply, she went on, "Boy, what a storm! It is so, so scary out there. My father said we're really in for it."

"What is that supposed to mean?" asked Pamela.

"It means we are in great danger," said Nancy in a low voice.

Even Pamela looked scared at that.

Then I said, "Maybe this is a good time for Charlie to tell us a ghost story. He promised he would."

"Ooh," said Leslie. "I don't know. . . ."

"Oh, it will only be fun scary," I told her. "Honest."

So I found Charlie, and we sat on the sleeping bags in the playroom again. Pamela started out on a chair. But as Charlie told the story, she began edging off of it.

Charlie's story was about a ghost that haunts a huge mansion. The people in the house only see him when it rains. The ghost wears a bucket on his head, so the family calls him Buckethead. This makes the ghost angry.

"I will get you! I will get revenge!" wails the ghost.

Pamela slid all the way off of her chair.

70

Now she was sitting on the floor.

I looked at Nancy. She was looking at me. Her eyes were shining. Very quietly, she reached over and turned off a lamp.

"Aughh!" shrieked everyone except Charlie and Nancy and me.

Pamela moved onto Jannie's sleeping bag.

"The people in the house," Charlie was saying, "heard clanking sounds . . . like chains being rattled. A girl saw a white figure standing at the end of her bed one night. The figure said, 'I will taaaake my reveeeenge soooooon.'"

"Ooh," whispered Hannie.

Outside, the wind howled. The rain beat on the windows. Just as Buckethead was taking his revenge, a bolt of lightning lit up the playroom.

Then the lights went out.

"Where Am I?"

"**H**elp! Oh, help!" Was that Pamela's voice? I couldn't be sure.

"Where am I? I can't see a thing!" cried someone else.

It was true. I held my hand in front of my face. I could not see it.

All around me, my friends were screaming. Some of them were even crying. I knew for sure that Natalie was crying, because she snorts when she cries.

"Calm down, you guys!" I heard Charlie

say. "We probably just blew a fuse or something. I'll go check the fuse box."

"No!" shrieked Natalie. (Snort, snort.) "No! Don't leave us!"

"How about if I send Kristy up here to stay with you?"

"That's fine," I replied, before Natalie could answer him.

In a few minutes I could see a light bobbing down the hallway.

"Eeeee! It's Buckethead!" cried Natalie. (Snort, snort.)

"Who's Buckethead?" That was Kristy. She was making the bobbing light. She was running through the hallway with a flashlight.

"That is my sister," I announced to my party guests. "Don't worry."

Kristy was carrying three more flashlights with her. She set them on the floor and turned them on. The room looked spooky and shadowy, but at least we could see again.

Natalie was still crying. Actually, she was

the only one crying. My other friends looked
scared but okay. Pamela found her chair
again.

"I'm frightened," wailed Natalie.

"Wimp," muttered Pamela.

"Did Charlie look at the fuse box?" I
asked Kristy.

"He didn't need to," she replied. "And
I'm afraid I have a little bit of bad news."

"Oh, no!" cried Natalie. (Snort.)

"What kind of bad news?" I asked.

"It's not a problem with our fuse box. There's a blackout. We looked outside. There are no lights on anywhere. That means nobody in our neighborhood has any power."

Natalie snorted and said she wanted to go home.

Pamela called her a wimp again.

Then Leslie said, "My big brother told me that thunder is really dead people bowling, and if a bowling ball rolls into the gutter, it will fall out of the sky. It could crash right through the roof of your house."

"*My* brother," began Jannie, "says that lightning is caused by angry ghosts. And if they're angry enough, they will send a lightning bolt right down to the ground."

Hannie began to cry then, too (at least she doesn't snort), so Kristy said, "Haven't you guys heard about cold fronts and warm fronts?"

In the dim light I saw Pamela yawn.

"Cold fronts and warm fronts?" Nancy repeated.

"Yes," said Kristy. "A thunderstorm is

just weather. That's *all*. When air is un-stable — like if it rises up instead of staying still — and if the air is wet, too, then you get a thunderstorm. See, the big, dark thunderclouds are charged with electricity. . . ."

"Do you know what she's talking about?" I heard Leslie whisper to Natalie.

"No." Natalie didn't even snort.

And at just that moment, the power returned. All the lights came on again.

"Hurray!" cheered my friends.

16

Bedtime

With the lights on again, the playroom looked very cheerful. My friends and I did not feel scared at all anymore.

"Do you guys know enough about thunderstorms now?" asked Kristy.

"Yes!" we cried.

"Because I could teach you some more things — "

"NO!" we shouted. We began to giggle.

Kristy left then. Jannie turned on her musical puppy. I tried to turn a cartwheel over the sleeping bags (I fell down), and

Nancy threw a stuffed toy at Hannie. Hannie shrieked and threw it back.

"Ahem!"

Uh-oh. That was Daddy. I could tell without even turning around.

Everyone stopped what they were doing.

"Girls?" said Daddy.

"Yes?" I sat up and looked at him.

"Bedtime now, okay? You've had plenty of excitement for one night."

I looked at my watch. It was only ten o'clock. My friends and I had planned to stay up until at least midnight. But all I said was, "All right. 'Night, Daddy. We'll get ready for bed now."

"Sleep tight, girls," said Daddy. Then he left.

My friends began groaning. They said things like, "Karen, we have to go to bed *now?*" And, "But, Karen, it's too *early!*"

Pamela said, "I go to bed at ten o'clock on *school* nights."

I smiled. "We're not *really* going to bed now. We are just going to pretend. We will put on our pajamas and get in our sleeping bags — "

"Or beds," interrupted Pamela.

"Whatever. Anyway," I went on, "then we will talk and tell stories until midnight. And *then* we are going to do something special. We will do it in the dark when Daddy and Elizabeth and everyone else in the house is asleep," I said very mysteriously.

"What is it?" whispered Hannie with wide eyes.

"Secret," I replied. "Now, come on. Let's get ready for bed before Daddy comes back and has to tell us a second time. Sometimes he gets mad if he has to tell me things twice."

So my friends and I put on our pajamas. Everyone agreed that Leslie's leopard-skin nightgown was the best. Pamela went into the bathroom. She washed her face. She brushed her teeth. The rest of us did not bother. We knew those things did not matter at a sleepover.

When she was finished, she stood in the doorway to the playroom.

"Are you *sure* you don't want to borrow my extra sleeping bag?" asked Nancy sweetly. "I brought it just for you."

"I am very sure," said Pamela.

I tried not to laugh. Instead I said, "Come on, Pamela. I will show you where my room is. I hope you like my bed."

Pamela and I walked down the hall to my room. Pamela was just about to climb into my bed when she stopped. "What are *those?*" she asked, pointing to the end of my bed.

"They are Tickly and Moosie," I told her.

"*Baby* things?" she asked, picking one up like it was a bug.

"No!" I exclaimed. I grabbed Tickly and Moosie. They would probably get cooties from Pamela.

"Do you still sleep with them?" asked Pamela.

I did not answer her. Pamela got into my bed.

"See you at midnight," I told her.

And since she was such a grown-up, I did not turn on my night-light or leave the door open a crack. I left her in pitch blackness. Then I returned to my friends. *They* would not make fun of my blanket or my stuffed cat.

Midnight

I had been afraid that staying awake until midnight might be hard. Last year, I tried to stay awake until midnight on New Year's Eve, but I could not do it. I fell asleep. Luckily, Mommy and Seth woke me up just in time to yell, "Hurray! Happy New Year!"

But at my sleepover, nobody had any trouble staying awake. Even with the lights out. The very first thing that happened after we were supposed to be asleep was that Nancy asked a question.

She said, "Who here likes Pamela?"

At first nobody said a word.

Then a girl named Sara said, "*I* like her. She is cool. She is so grown-up."

And Leslie said, "I wish I looked like her. I wish my mother would let me wear clothes like Pamela's."

Most of the girls wanted Pamela to like them. Or they wanted to be like her. But they didn't say they *liked Pamela*.

Finally Nancy said, "I think Pamela is a jerk."

Jannie gasped.

It was time to change the subject. "What," I began in a low voice, "is the scariest thing that has ever happened to anyone here?"

"Getting lost at Disney World," said Natalie right away.

"That happened to me once, too!" I exclaimed.

We told scary stories and funny stories and embarrassing stories for a long, long time. Finally I turned on one of the flashlights that Kristy had brought to the playroom. I looked at my watch.

"Hey, you guys! It's almost midnight!" I said in a loud whisper.

"You better go get Pamela," said Sara.

"Oh," I groaned, but I tiptoed to my room anyway. I opened the door. "Hey, Pamela," I said. "It's almost midnight. It is time for the secret surprise."

No answer. I shined the flashlight in Pamela's face. She was sound asleep. I decided to leave her that way. She probably needed her beauty rest.

I went back to the playroom and told my friends I could not wake up Pamela. Then I said, "Guess what. Now it is time to . . . raid the refrigerator!"

"Yea!" yelled a couple of girls.

"SHHH!" I hissed. "We have to be very quiet, and we cannot turn on any lamps."

I passed around the flashlights and we tiptoed downstairs. On the way, Jannie crashed into a table. We were all quiet for a few moments, but I did not hear Daddy or Elizabeth getting up. So we went toward the kitchen.

85

When we got there, we had to leave the light off.

"We do not want anyone to know we are awake," I reminded my friends.

Then we opened the refrigerator. There was leftover apple pie and bread and lots of stuff for making sandwiches. There was fruit and juice and soda and milk.

"Help yourselves!" I said.

But just then I heard a low growl. I looked at the doorway to the kitchen. Floating in the air was a glowing monster head. It did not have a body.

"Aughh!" I shrieked.

"Aughh!" shrieked my friends.

The monster turned on a lamp. It was just Sam. He was shining a flashlight behind a scary mask.

"Sam!" I exclaimed.

"What is going on here?" (Uh-oh. That was Daddy.) "Everybody back to bed," he said. "And I mean it."

So we went to bed for real this time. We did not get to raid the refrigerator.

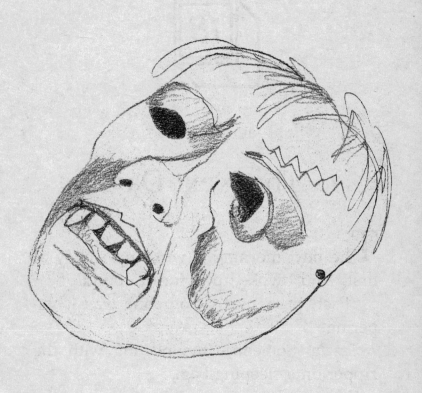

The Next Day

The next morning, I woke up slowly at first. And I woke up to funny sounds.

"Psst, psst, psst." Someone was whispering.

Zzzzip. Someone was playing with the zipper on a sleeping bag.

Creeeak. Someone was tiptoeing across the room.

Who *are* all these people? I thought. And why are they in my bedroom? Then I remembered the sleepover. The people were my friends, and I was in the playroom in a sleeping bag on the floor. Suddenly I was wide awake.

"Morning!" I said, sitting up.

"Morning," replied Hannie, cheerfully. "Guess what time it is."

"Seven-thirty?" I asked.

"Nope. Ten o'clock."

"Ten o'clock!" I cried. "We've wasted half the morning! Everybody get up. It's breakfast time. It's almost *lunch*time!"

Soon my friends and I were up and dressed. We cleaned the playroom. We rolled up our sleeping bags. Then I had to go get Pamela before we went downstairs.

"Where are your blanky and aminal?" she asked in a baby voice.

"Never mind," I replied.

My friends and I went into the kitchen. Daddy and Nannie were there.

"Well, here are the sleepyheads," said Nannie, smiling.

And Daddy said, "How about a picnic breakfast in the backyard?"

I looked outside. I remembered the storm

the night before. But now the sun was shining and the sky was blue.

"Okay!" I said. "Thanks, Daddy."

The ground was still wet from the rain, so we spread out plastic mats. Then we put blankets over them. Nannie made pancakes and bacon, and then Daddy helped us carry our plates outside. We were starving. We ate two helpings of everything — except for Leslie, who does not like pancakes. (She is the only person I know who does not like

them.) And except for Nancy. She did not eat any bacon. She never eats pork.

"Why?" asked Jannie.

"Because my family is Jewish," Nancy replied. "And Mommy and Daddy say, 'No pork.' I do not like bacon anyway."

We were just finishing our breakfast when we heard a car horn. Someone had pulled up in front of the big house.

"Karen!" Elizabeth called. "Jannie's mother is here." So Jannie had to leave.

I wished very hard that the next parent who arrived would be one of Pamela's. My wish came true. Mr. Harding arrived next. Pamela gathered up her things. It took her a long time, even though she did not have a sleeping bag. I was not sorry to see Pamela go. She had been gigundo mean about Moosie, Tickly, and a lot of other things. I decided I did not want to be Pamela's friend, no matter what.

I wanted to tell her those things.

But I did not do it. Not in front of the other girls.

All I said was, " 'Bye, Pamela. Thanks for coming. See you in school!"

I heaved a huge sigh of relief.

Then I turned to smile at Hannie and Nancy.

The Three Musketeers

Pretty soon, everyone was gone — everyone except Hannie and Nancy. Hannie lived so close by that she could walk home. We did not know where Nancy's parents were but we hoped they were at home. We wanted to ask them if Nancy could spend the day at the big house. Hannie already had permission.

Guess what. We called the Dawses and they were still at home. They said it would be okay for Mommy to take her home when she picked up Andrew and me that afternoon.

So the three of us had a whole day to spend together.

"Boy, am I glad you guys aren't fighting anymore," said Hannie to Nancy and me.

"I'm glad, too," said Nancy and I at the same time.

Then Nancy said, "Remember when you and Hannie were mad at each other?"

"Yup," I replied, and added, "Remember when *you* and Hannie were mad at each other?"

"Yup," said Nancy.

"Boy, we should stop fighting," I said. "We are lucky we are friends. If we were not friends, we might have to be friends with Pamela."

"Oh, yuck," said Nancy to Hannie.

"You know what?" I said. "We are like the Three Musketeers."

"Hey!" cried Nancy. "I've got a great idea. We should become blood sisters!"

"Blood sisters?" repeated Hannie.

94

"Yeah," said Nancy. "We prick our fingers. Then when the blood comes out, we mix it all up so we each have a little of our friends' blood."

"Ew!" cried Hannie. "That sounds gross."

"We could try it anyway," I said.

I wasn't sure that this was a good idea. Even so, I found a needle. I washed it off with alcohol so it would be clean. Then I handed it to Nancy. "You go first," I told her.

"Prick my *own* finger? No way!" she exclaimed.

"Well, don't prick mine," said Hannie, "I really don't think we should mix up our blood. Even if it would make us blood sisters."

"Don't look at me," I said to Nancy. "I do not want you to stick me, either. I do not think it is safe."

"Neither do I," said Nancy finally.

So in the end we decided to be just the Three Musketeers, not blood sisters.

We wrote up a pact. It looked like this:

WE ARE THE THREE MUSKETEERS
WE VOW TO BE FRIENDS FOR LIFE.
SIGNED,
Karen Brewer
Nancy Dawes
Hannie Papadakis

School Again

"Look. Look at my new outfit!" said Pamela Harding.

It was Monday. It was the day after Nancy and Hannie and I became the Three Musketeers. We were in school again, and Pamela was prancing around our classroom. She was wearing a bright green dress made of sweat shirt material, black tights, and over the tights, green push-down socks. But best of all, on her feet were high-topped moccasins with fringe.

I bet you could smell her sister's perfume

a mile away. I could smell it in the back of the room, and Pamela was in the front.

"Pamela?" said Jannie. "Maybe you could come over to my house after school some day."

"I want you to come ice-skating with me," said Sara.

I looked at the two other Musketeers. "Don't Jannie and Sara remember how awful Pamela was at the sleepover?" I asked them.

"I guess not," answered Nancy, "but I do not care. If those girls want to be friends with Pamela, then let them."

"Yeah," said Hannie. "We have each other. We are the Three Musketeers now."

"Oh, Hannie! We have your copy of the pact," I said.

The night before, Nancy and I had given the pact to Nancy's daddy. Mr. Dawes had made two copies of it on his copy machine at home. One copy was for Nancy and one was for Hannie. I kept the real pact, the one we had actually signed.

"Thanks," said Nancy, when I gave her the copy.

Then Nancy pulled her copy out of the pocket of her jeans. I pulled the real pact out of my knapsack.

We read the pact aloud together.

"We are the Three Musketeers. We vow to be friends for life."

"Maybe," I said, watching Pamela, "we should add something to our pact. Something like, 'And we vow never to be friends with Pamela Harding.'"

"I like our pact the way it is," said Hannie. She was reading hers again.

"Who cares about Pamela, anyway?" asked Nancy.

"*They* do," I replied. I pointed to the girls who had surrounded Pamela. Pamela was showing off every inch of her outfit.

I wondered if the girls were more impressed with Pamela or her clothes. And then something occurred to me. The girls in the class liked Pamela's glamor. But they did not know the real Pamela that was underneath. Would they find out? If they did find out and they did not like her, would they care?

Well, I knew one thing. Even if Pamela became Queen of the Classroom, the Three Musketeers would stick together. I said so to Hannie and Nancy.

"Right," said Hannie.

"Through thick and thin," said Nancy.

"Forever and ever," I added.

We invented a secret Three Musketeers handshake. We clapped our hands once, we made a tower out of our fists, then we snapped our fingers twice. It was gigundo cool.

"Hi!" said Natalie Springer just then. She joined my friends and me in the back of the room. She had left the crowd around Pamela. "You know what?" she said to me. "Your sleepover was the best ever. Even though I have never been to one before."

Ricky came over to us, too. "Hey," he said. "I heard your sleepover was really

fun. Can I come to the next one?"

"Maybe," I said, smiling.

And when Natalie and Ricky were gone, us Three Musketeers did our secret handshake again.

About the Author

ANN M. MARTIN lives in New York City and loves animals. Her cat, Mouse, knows how to take the phone off the hook.

Other books by Ann M. Martin that you might enjoy are *Stage Fright, Me and Katie (the Pest)*, and the books in *The Baby-sitters Club* series.

Ann likes ice cream, the beach, and *I Love Lucy*. And she has her own little sister, whose name is Jane.

Little Sister

Don't miss #10

KAREN'S GRANDMOTHERS

"Our class has been given a special honor," said Ms. Colman. "We've been chosen to 'adopt' some of the people at Stoneybrook Manor. Anyone who is interested will be assigned to a resident. You'll visit your new 'grandparent' twice a week after school. It will mean a lot to the people there. Some of them don't have any visitors at all. They are very lonely. Who would like to adopt a grandparent?"

I raised my hand right away. (So did Ricky and Hannie and several other kids.) Here's the thing. My parents are divorced. Then they each got married again. So I have *four* grandmothers — two regular ones, and two stepgrandmothers. If I adopted a fifth grandma, I would break the grandmother record for good!

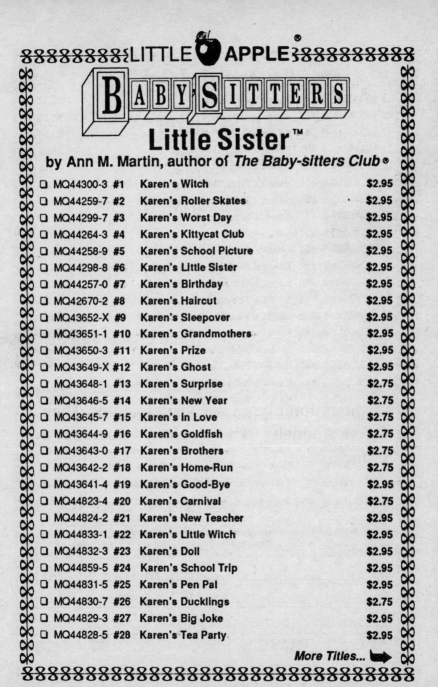

LITTLE APPLE

BABY-SITTERS
Little Sister™
by Ann M. Martin, author of *The Baby-sitters Club*

More Titles... ➡